Julia

Diary

Book 4

My First Boyfriend

Katrina Kahler

Copyright © KC Global Enterprises

All Rights Reserved

Table of Contents

Standing tall...

Her blazing eyes glared in my direction. I could feel the intense hatred as she stared at me. What was going on? What had I done to deserve this? I thought the stupid bullying stuff was behind us.

In that moment, I knew that we would never be friends and I was better off without her. There was no way that she was ever going to let this go. But what was I going to do? Just let her walk all over me. Let her win out, yet again?

No! I decided right then. It was not going to happen. I knew how to deal with people like her. I had done it before and I could do it again.

"Stand tall, Julia!" I said to myself. "She is not better than you! Show her that! Let her know that you believe in yourself!"

Taking a deep breath, I repeated in my mind once more, "I can do this! I am a confident person. I deserve respect!" And with a self-assured toss of my head, I threw my shoulders back and strode confidently past her.

The look of disgust on her face did nothing to sway my resolve. I ignored her evil stare and continued on, an image of confidence.

"No one is going to bully me!" That is the message I wanted to convey and even though I was shaking inside, I felt good. I felt proud. And I continued on my way.

"If this is a contest, then I am the winner," I thought firmly to myself.

With a smile on my face, I walked towards the most amazing person in my life right then and added my name to the list.

One month earlier…

"Do you want to go out with me, Julia?"

Blake's sweet smile made my heart melt and hearing those words caused my own smile to become wider than ever. The fluttery feeling in my stomach sent tingles down my spine and I pictured the look on Millie's face when I told her the news.

Blake Jansen wanted me to go out with him. Not just once to the movies, but really go out, as in hanging out together at school every day and maybe even on the weekends. It was another dream come true and I clasped my hands together in delight as I pictured all the wonderful times we would share. I could see him carrying my books into class and reserving a seat for me in the lunch area. I could also see the look of envy on all the other girls' faces.

As he reached over to hold my hand, I felt my stomach drop. I looked into his eyes and held his gaze, smiling shyly. Then, beaming with pride, I opened my mouth to respond to the question I had been longing to hear.

"Yes, Blake. I would love to!" The words were just about to come spilling out when the wonderful image I had created was suddenly and unexpectedly wiped clear from my mind.

"Julia! What is wrong with you? Are you going deaf or something? I called you about five times. Why didn't you answer me?" The look of annoyance on my brother's face along with his angry tone snapped my mind back to reality.

"What are you doing in here anyway? I need you to come downstairs and help me clean up the mess in the kitchen. Mom will be home soon and she'll freak out if those dirty dishes are still piled up in the sink."

"Alright, I'm coming!" I replied with frustration. Matt's timing was unbelievable. Right in the middle of the best daydream I have ever had and he comes barging into my room to get me to help clean up the kitchen.

"Can't you just clean it up?" I snapped. "Do I have to help you do everything?"

"I did it last time and besides, I've been invited to Jack's party tonight and I don't want to give Mom any excuses to stop me from going. You promised me that you'd help!"

I rolled my eyes at him as I reluctantly hopped off my bed where I'd been laying blissfully only moments before. Trudging down the stairs, I followed him towards the kitchen. He had been giving Mom and Dad a lot of attitude recently and so they'd decided to ground him for two weeks to try and teach him a lesson. However, as the two weeks were almost up and he had been doing his best to behave himself, Mom promised that he could go to the party if all the chores were done when she got home from work. And typical of my brother, Matt, he had left the kitchen until the last minute and was now panicking that it wouldn't be cleaned up in time.

As I wiped down the bench top, fleeting thoughts of the wonderful daydream I had been having, appeared once more in my mind.

It had been the best daydream ever and I still couldn't believe that it had been interrupted by Matt, just so I could help him clean up the kitchen!

Sighing, I put the last dirty plate in the dishwasher and turned it on.

Jimmy...

Blake and I have been hanging out a bit over the summer break and I have the feeling that he really likes me. I know with certainty that I definitely like him! We did go out to the movies one night on a kind of date but since then, he hasn't mentioned that "date" word again. I think it's probably because he's too shy.

And there's no way, I'm going to ask him to go out with me. I mean, it's up to the boys to do the asking, isn't it? That's what Millie and I think, anyway. But as far as Blake is concerned, it's not only that he's very cute looking but he's a really nice boy as well. He doesn't have the stuck up attitude of all the cool boys at school. Not that Blake isn't cool, because he is, he just doesn't act like the others.

One more week left until school goes back to start the new school year and I know my friends will be so jealous if they hear that Blake and I are actually girlfriend and boyfriend. That's not the reason that I'm keen to go out with him though. I do genuinely really like him. I've kind of had crushes on other boys before, but nothing like this.

I remember when I was in fourth grade and there was this boy called Jimmy Wakefield. I thought he was the cutest boy I had ever seen. We'd actually been at school together since kindergarten but it took until fourth grade for me to notice him. He had this flicked back hairstyle that was so in fashion then and he was also really funny. He was probably one of the most popular kids in the class and I had the biggest crush. But I wasn't the only one who felt that way. Probably just about every other girl in my class liked him as well. Then one day, I realized that even though he was super good looking, he was not really a nice person at all.

I watched him let his best friend take all the blame for

something that he was actually responsible for. I saw it happen with my own eyes and I still can't believe that Jimmy did what he did!

There was another boy in our class named Reece and he had brought in a really cool compass that he'd been given for his birthday. Everyone loved it, in particular the boys, and many of them thought that it was the coolest thing they had ever seen. It had a flip-up cover that opened by pressing a small button on the side and it also glowed in the dark. I think the most distinctive thing about it though was that it had a heap of special effects. It even had an inbuilt torch that you could change to a laser light with the flick of a little switch. It really was the coolest looking compass and everyone was desperate to have a turn of using it.

Apparently, Reece's dad had bought it for him while he was traveling overseas and no one had seen one like it anywhere before. That's what made it so appealing.

Reece had been allowed to bring it to school for show and tell, although our teacher really didn't like us bringing stuff like that in. First of all, it took up lots of time when she said that we should be focusing on school work and as well as that, she didn't like the idea of expensive items like that being at school. Anyway, after we came in from lunch break, Jimmy realized that his compass was missing. He had left it on the teacher's desk for safekeeping but when he asked her for it back, it was nowhere to be seen.

Our teacher, who was named Miss Bromley, asked everyone to check inside their desks just in case it had accidentally ended up in there somehow. I could tell that she didn't want to create a fuss and start blaming kids for stealing. I guess her main aim was to simply get Reece's compass back. She told us that if we found it, to return it and the problem would be solved without anyone getting into trouble.

Unfortunately, though, no one admitted to finding it or knowing of its whereabouts.

So Miss Bromley decided to check everyone's desks herself. Just as she turned down my row I happened to spot Jimmy, who sat at the desk in front of me, very secretly slip something into the desk of the boy sitting next to him. Now it just so happened that this boy, called Ryan was Jimmy's best friend. At the time, I didn't think too much of it. That was until Miss Bromley checked Ryan's desk and actually found the compass staring at her, the minute she checked. I knew without any doubt that Jimmy had put it there. I sat right behind him and had a clear view of the entire incident. And I knew that I wasn't mistaken.

The look of shock on Ryan's face was proof that he knew nothing about it, but Jimmy had just sat innocently by and let his best friend take the blame for stealing. That's what he was accused of, and even though Ryan denied it, Miss Bromley did not believe him and he got into heaps of trouble.

I was convinced that I should tell Miss Bromley what had really happened but I felt way too shy to speak up. Back then, I rarely even put my hand up in class, let alone possess the courage to tell on one of my classmates. And especially to tell on someone who everyone thought was the coolest kid in the entire grade as well as being someone I had a huge crush on! For a long time afterward, I was overcome with guilt about that day. I knew deep down that I should have spoken up about it but I didn't. And looking back, I still feel so ashamed, even now.

After that incident, I changed my mind about Jimmy completely. My crush melted away into oblivion and I wondered how I could ever have thought that he was so cool. I mean who would do something like that to their best friend? It was so horrible!

It really taught me a lesson as well! Just because someone is cool and good looking, doesn't mean that they're a nice person!

And that's one of the reasons I like Blake so much. I know in my heart that he would never treat his friends badly.

As I wiped the last crumb off the kitchen bench, thoughts of Blake lingered in my mind. Suddenly, I focused on the weekend ahead and the music camp that was planned. Blake was going to be there and it just couldn't come quickly enough.

Music camp…

Saturday dawned bright and clear and I was up early with all my gear packed and ready. My guitar stood in its case right by the front door, next to my pillow, sleeping bag and carry bag that contained all my clothes and the bits and pieces I would need for the following 3 days.

The camp is an annual event and the aim is to teach and inspire young kids who are talented at singing or playing some kind of musical instrument. You have to be at a reasonable level to attend and the kids who went last year all raved about how much fun it was and how much they had improved after the time they'd spent there. Blake and I had both signed up to go and I couldn't wait.

I'd barely been able to sleep the night before. I just love anything to do with dancing and music, whether it's simply dancing, playing an instrument or listening to music. I love it all!!

I was also really looking forward to being with a group of other musical kids and in particular of course, I was most looking forward to hanging out with Blake. Although I knew that I would enjoy it regardless, it would obviously be so much more fun to have Blake there too.

As Dad and I pulled out of the driveway, I waved goodbye to Mom who was standing at the front door, watching us leave. Dad was one of the few parents who had volunteered to attend and I was very grateful for that. Without the help of those few parents, the camp would not have been able to go ahead.

Driving down the highway towards the campground which was only a few kilometers from where I lived, I thought back over the events that had led to that moment. Being given my guitar by my best friend, Millie was one of the biggest and most wonderful surprises I had ever experienced. And hardly a day had gone by where I had not picked it up from the spot where it sat right by my bed. Gradually I had improved and I was now keen to become better than ever.

I couldn't wait to go back to school and show Mr. Casey, my guitar teacher, how much my level of playing had developed. At the end of last semester, he had invited me to join one of the bands that he'd put together. The plan was for Blake to be the drummer and the two of us were really keen to get started. I definitely wanted to be as good as possible by then.

The look of excitement on my face as I focused on the weekend ahead must have been obvious because Dad commented with a quick grin, "We're almost there, Julia! You've been waiting all summer for this camp and now the time has finally arrived!"

"I know," I squealed, unable to contain the enthusiasm I was feeling. "I can't wait to get there!"

And just as those words were out of my mouth, Dad indicated to the left and took the turn that led down the long, narrow driveway to the campground.

Lots of cars were arriving and several kids and their parents were milling about, waiting for instructions. Leaping from the car as it pulled to a stop, I spotted a girl from my grade standing nearby. I'd had no idea that anyone else from school apart from Blake and I, were attending and I was really pleased to see another familiar face.

"Hi, Suzy!" I called out to her. "It's such a great surprise to see you here!"

Her friendly smile showed that she was just as pleased to see me. "Let's head to the girls' dorm and unpack our stuff!" I suggested eagerly, noticing the sign that led to the girls' sleeping cabins.

Chatting excitedly, we grabbed our gear and headed off. My dad had gone in the direction of the office to see what he could do to help with the general organization for the weekend and I told him that I would see him a bit later.

As we rounded the corner of the building and approached the doorway, I reached out to turn the doorknob and then pushed on the door to open it. Unexpectedly, it kind of gave way and I fell forward. As I regained my footing, I looked up just in time to prevent myself from bumping heads with the person who had pulled the door open from the other side.

When recognition dawned and I realized that the individual in front of me was not just a vision but was actually really there in the flesh, I gasped involuntarily and stood in stunned silence.

Unable to hide the shock I felt at seeing the familiar figure standing there, I opened my mouth to speak, but words failed to appear.

"Hi, Julia!" her sweet smile did nothing to dispel the dismay that had engulfed me like the sudden blow of a sledgehammer.

"Sara!" I exclaimed. "I didn't know that you were coming this weekend!"

"It was really last minute," she replied, a look of assured confidence on her face. "Apparently one of the girls canceled and a spot opened up. My mom just happened to hear about it all and booked me in."

"And I didn't know that you played an instrument?" I continued to query, trying to overcome the shock I was still feeling.

"I don't," she replied, smugly. "I like to sing. I've always been too shy to sing in public but Mom finally convinced me that I should. She's always going on about how good I am. You know what mothers are like though. I'm really not that good."

I looked at her unconvinced, never knowing Sara to be genuinely modest and then I remembered that Suzy was standing there and Sara hadn't even acknowledged her.

"Do you know Suzy?" I asked. "She's in our grade at school."

"Oh hello, Suzy," Sara responded. "Yes, I remember seeing you around the school. This is going to be so much fun, especially now that there are three of us here from our grade. Well, I've been asked to help the camp organizers, so I had better get moving. Just go straight through that doorway and you'll find the girls' dorm."

"Oh, one more thing; there's only one double bed and I've already claimed it," she continued with a smirk. "Bad luck girls, first in first served!"

Indicating a nearby door, she gave a small but confident wave and took off down the pathway.

Looking towards Suzy with a disbelieving shake of my head and a huge sigh, I exclaimed, "Well, I was not expecting Sara to be here, that's for sure!"

Questioningly, Suzy raised her eyebrows in response but I decided quickly that I should take control of my senses and try not to let Sara's presence dampen my enthusiasm.

"Come on," I said with a sudden resolve, "Let's go and unpack!" And with a firm stride, I led the way into the girls' dorm to select a bed. I'd been looking forward to this camp all summer long and I was not going to let anything spoil it, especially not Sara Hamilton!

Tug-Of-War...

After unpacking all our gear, everyone assembled in the large meeting room. I scanned all the unfamiliar faces hoping to spot Blake's, but he was nowhere to be seen. I began to worry that something might have happened to him. It was unlike him to be late and he should definitely have already arrived.

The camp mentors had arranged for us to be organized into groups according to our ability level and instrument. We were given instructions for the morning and told to meet in the dining room for lunch. I then made my way with a group of other guitarists to a nearby practice area. Our mentor, who was named Andy, was really cool. He was kind of hippy looking with long wispy hair and wore a vest that had fringing hanging down the back.

Apparently, he was the lead guitarist in a local band and I could see that he was exceptionally good. Turning his amplifier up, he unexpectedly blasted us with some incredible lead guitar. He then spent time teaching us some new riffs and I was really pleased as I was able to pick up what he was showing us, super quickly.

The morning passed by in what seemed the blink of an eye and before we knew it, it was time to head to the dining area for lunch. Just as I was about to sit down, my plate overflowing with the biggest burger I think I had ever seen in my entire life, I spotted Blake's familiar figure walking through the door. Almost instantly, we made eye contact and I felt my stomach flutter with relief that he had arrived safely.

"Blake!" I called out excitedly. And just as I was about to beckon him over to the spare seat beside me, Sara jumped up and raced to his side.

Grabbing hold of his hand, she dragged him to her table and

stuck a huge plate of food right in front of him. From where I was sitting, I had an unobstructed view and I watched her whole face light up with the excitement of having him right beside her.

He threw an apologetic look my way and indicated that he would eat his lunch and then come over. Meanwhile, I sighed with disappointment as I stared down at the burger in front of me. I had suddenly lost my appetite and really did not feel like eating anymore.

"Why did Sara have to come?" I thought to myself as I scanned the room once again.

"There are so many more boys here than girls and she could probably get the attention of any one of them. Why does she have to zone in on Blake?" I shook my head in dismay as thoughts of Sara filled my mind.

Then, tired of waiting, I took a deep breath and made my way over to where they were sitting. I had decided to just be myself and not make a big deal of things. I knew that Blake was my friend and nothing would get in the way of that, not even Sara's pretty face and overpowering personality.

However, the minute Sara saw me approaching, she quickly jumped to her feet and tugged on Blake's hand in a possessive and self-assured manner.

"Come on Blake," she said to him eagerly. "I'll show you where the boys' dorm is so you can unpack your gear."

But to my huge delight, Blake shrugged off Sara's firm grasp of his hand and stood up to greet me.

"Julia!" his broad smile caused the familiar flutter inside me to return, the one I seemed to be overcome with whenever he was nearby. It then tingled right down my spine as he gave me one of his friendly big hugs.

I couldn't help but notice the look of disgust on Sara's face but she managed to conceal it with a false grin when Blake looked her way once more.

"Let's all head over to the dorms," Blake said tactfully. "I got held up this morning because my mom's car wouldn't start and we had to wait for the road service guy to come and get it going again. But now, I'm just keen to put my gear away and start playing some music."

Smiling in his usual friendly manner, Blake chatted on as we walked towards the dorms. He seemed oblivious of Sara's demands on his attention. Although, I wasn't sure if he really was aware of what was going on or just pretending not to notice.

But feeling more confident, I also focused on ignoring her annoying behavior and looked forward to the afternoon ahead. The plan was to do another session with our mentors and then get together for a combined session after dinner. The mentors had said that they were going to select different kids from each group to form bands and the night times would be used to practice for the final performance on the last day. It would kind of be like a Battle of the Bands competition and the winning group would win some recording time in a studio.

Looking forward to the evening session with excited anticipation, I left Blake to unpack and walked with Sara back towards our rehearsal rooms. At least she was in a different group to me, so I could simply enjoy playing guitar and improving my skills, which was the reason I was there in the first place. Of course, having Blake around was an added bonus but I decided to focus on guitar, for the afternoon anyway.

"Hopefully Blake and I will be put into the same band and then we can just catch up during rehearsals tonight," I thought happily to myself.

Little did I know, however, that Sara had the same thoughts running through her mind as well.

Dreaming…

The afternoon session passed by quickly and before we knew it, everyone was heading to the dining room for dinner. I grabbed a table and Suzy and I managed to save some spots. When I saw Blake enter, I waved him towards us. Not far behind was Sara of course, and beaming widely, she walked over and sat down next to him.

"Oh my gosh," she seemed so excited, she could barely speak. "I've had the most amazing afternoon. My mentor, Johnny, who is really, really cute by the way, thinks that I have an incredible voice. Can you believe it!! I'm absolutely buzzing right now. This could be the beginning of my career as a singer."

"Wow, Sara!" Blake exclaimed. "That's so awesome. I can't wait to hear you sing."

"Oh wow!" I also exclaimed, feeling a twinge of envy. I then forced myself to add, "You'll have to sing for us tonight."

"But I'm so shy!" she replied. "I'm not sure I can sing in front of a big audience!"

I could not help but roll my eyes at her comment. "Sara, you are definitely not shy! I'm sure you'll be fine."

"Well, I hope so!" she beamed, not looking the slightest bit concerned about being shy. "Having my friends here will make it so much easier," she continued, smiling sweetly at each of us.

Suzy gave me a funny look just then. I kind of got the feeling that she was starting to see what Sara was really like. But I brushed thoughts of her behavior aside and we all settled into our meal. However, looking at Sara's pretty face across the table, a kind of strange premonition crossed my mind and I couldn't help but wonder what was ahead. I had been through so much with Sara already and I wondered what she had planned.

A feeling of unease started to trickle down my spine as I scraped another spoonful of food from my plate.

***

Heading into the performance room after dinner, I decided to shake all negative thoughts aside and focus on enjoying the night. We were going to be put into different groups and asked to perform together, which I found quite nerve-wracking but exciting at the same time. Visions of being a rock star flashed through my mind. That was one of my secret dreams and the image I had formed in my head made me dizzy with the thrill of such a possibility ever happening.

I knew that even a year earlier, I would have thought such an idea was crazy but now I understand that dreams really can come true and I've since added this to my list of goals for the future. I mean lots of kids become superstars, so why can't it happen to me? With some hard work and persistence, maybe I can make that dream a reality!

Totally unexpected…

When we were all assembled in the performance room, the first group of kids was sent to an area where a mentor was waiting to help them work together as a band. The rest of us sat anxiously, wondering who we had been teamed up with. We kind of wished we could form our own bands but we'd been told that we needed to be grouped together with kids of a similar level and style.

As I sat with my fingers crossed, the names I'd hope to hear were announced over the microphone. "Julia Jones on lead guitar, Brodie Sanders on bass, Blake Jansen on drums and Suzy Bartlett as the singer."

"Yesss!" I squealed, unable to withhold my excitement. Blake and I high-fived each other and stood to make our way to the back of the room. But just then the microphone crackled once more.

"Sorry guys, I made a mistake," Andy, the mentor said apologetically. "Suzy, we actually think you'd be better with a different group of kids who are more suited to your singing style. Sara Hamilton, you're the one who we've decided would fit best with Julia and the others."

My mouth dropped wide open in shock at this announcement. "Noooooo!"

I screamed the unspoken word wildly in my mind as I watched Sara race over to Blake and throw her arms around him in total delight. This really couldn't be happening!

I glanced in despair towards Suzy, the frown on my face betraying my feelings.

"I wish we had you as our singer, Suzy!" I whispered dejectedly in her ear.

"Yeah, me too, Julia! That would have been so much fun." Looking as disappointed as I felt, she headed off in the opposite direction.

Typical of her usual style, the minute we sat down together, Sara was bursting with ideas and couldn't wait to share them with everyone else.

"There are so many great songs we can do that will suit my voice," she declared. "I actually have a list prepared, so how about we get started on these straight away." Pulling the list from her pocket she held it out for us all to see.

Just as I was about to speak, Andy, our mentor congratulated her for being so organized and keen. "This is great, Sara!" he exclaimed. "I love to see kids taking initiative. I'll download the music for some of these songs now and we'll see how you all go."

Before long, we were underway and even though I hated to admit it to myself, the songs that Sara had selected were pretty good. What I hadn't been prepared for though was the quality of her voice. She sings very well and if I was going to be totally honest with myself, she sings better than well. She is quite amazing and the boys obviously thought so too because they were giving her nonstop praise.

"Sara! Your voice is awesome!" Blake's response was genuinely sincere and I could see that he was really excited at having such an incredible singer for our band.

Brodie quickly agreed with him and it was clear that they were both very happy with how things were progressing. Their comments, along with the praise from Andy, boosted Sara's confidence even further and before long she had turned up the volume on her microphone and everyone was looking in our direction with open admiration at the sound of her voice.

I knew that I should feel proud to be part of such a talented group. Andy had given me some tricky lead guitar to play and the boys thought that it was really cool to have a girl guitarist, especially one who could play so well. But rather than feeling honored, I was overcome with a sick feeling in the pit of my stomach.

"Here we go again," I thought to myself. And as I watched Sara and Blake completely absorbed in each other and the sound that they were creating, I could not shake the uneasy sensation that this was not going to turn out the way I had imagined.

The accident…

The next day followed the same pattern as the one before and I was glad to be able to focus on my guitar playing without the distraction of Sara in my midst. I had noticed, however, that she was spending every spare minute trying to get Blake's attention. Just like a bee buzzing around a beehive, she barely left his side. And the way she flitted around him was sickening. I knew it was jealousy on my part, but I was having difficulty getting it under control.

After lunch, though, I saw that Blake had teamed up with a few kids to play guitar, but Sara was nowhere to be seen. Blake is so talented! Even though he's an awesome drummer, he's actually pretty good on the guitar and before long a group of kids was sitting with him, singing songs while he played.

During that time, I had decided to take the opportunity to have a one on one lesson with Andy. I was determined to really impress everyone with some lead guitar that I'd been working on. I thought it would be so cool to become a really good lead guitarist as you don't see many girls who actually excel at that. It's usually boys. But there's this famous girl guitarist whose video clips I've watched on YouTube and I've decided that she's my inspiration. I'd love to be able to play as well as her one day!

After finishing my lesson, I'd planned to join Blake and the others who were still sitting on the grass together, but just as I stood up to join them, Sara suddenly appeared and grabbed Blake by the hand. I stayed transfixed, wondering what she was up to. Then I saw her pull him in the direction of the swimming pool.

"I wonder if they're going swimming," I thought to myself, knowing that the pool was out of bounds unless there was an adult to supervise. Then just as I decided to head over towards them, Andy called me inside to help set up some gear for the rehearsals later that evening. To my disappointment, by the time we'd finished the sun was starting to set and everyone was beginning to fill the dining room in time for dinner.

Looking around, I could see no sign of Blake or Sara and wondered why they'd taken so long to come back.

Spotting Suzy, Brodie, and a few of the other kids who we had become friends with, I asked if they knew what had happened to them.

"I saw them down around the swimming pool a bit earlier," snickered Jack, a surly type of kid who was sitting nearby and had heard my question. He flicked back his long black fringe and looked at me with a kind of smirk. His hair was so jet black, I was sure that it was dyed and he had several piercings in his ears. His outfit consisted of a black T-shirt and black skinny jeans, which he even wore through the middle of the day when it was very hot. And his skin was so pale, I was sure that he rarely went out in the sun.

To his credit though, he was a very good guitarist. I think that was all he lived for and he probably stayed indoors all day, constantly playing guitar.

Ignoring him, I sat down in the spare seat that Suzy had saved for me and tried to join in the conversation. They were discussing the different songs that they'd planned to play for the concert the following night. All the parents were coming to watch and that was when we were going to perform the 'Battle of the Bands' which everyone was super excited about.

Intently, I looked around, scanning the room for signs of Blake or Sara, my anxiety growing with every second. I caught my dad's eye and gave him a wave. I had been so busy that I had hardly seen him throughout the entire weekend.

It had become quite dark outside and I was just on the verge of alerting one of the camp leaders that they were missing when Blake came running into the room. I saw him quickly glance towards me as he sprinted over to my dad and spoke to him in a very agitated manner.

Filled with concern, I raced across the dining room towards them. By this time though, Dad had leaped from his seat and was following Blake out the door.

As I ran after them, I called out to Blake but he had either chosen to ignore me or hadn't heard my voice and kept racing down the pathway in the direction of the swimming pool.

Dad had grabbed a torch on his way out and was shining it along the path to light their way. By that time, it was pitch black out there and very difficult to see the path.

Panting, I had to quicken my steps to keep up with them and continued on past the swimming pool area and along a track that led into the bush. My heart thumping, I finally managed to catch them, and in the dark, I almost ran right into Blake, whose dark colored T-shirt was camouflaged with the surroundings.

It was then that I heard the unmistakable sound of Sara's voice. "This way!" Blake called as he charged along the winding dirt track.

Following the sound of his steps and the dim beam of the torchlight, I made my way through the dense bushland and found Sara sitting on the ground, leaning awkwardly against a tree trunk.

"Blake!" she called out. "Thank goodness you're back. You took so long; I was beginning to get worried."

"Oh, Mr. Jones!" she cried. "Thank you so much for coming to get me! And Julia! You came too!" Her look of surprise at seeing me there was quickly whipped away when she tried to stand. Wincing with pain, she gratefully took the offer of support from Blake and my father.

"What happened?" I asked, frowning with curiosity but also concern. "And what were you doing out here anyway?"

"Well, I found this really cool track and Blake and I wanted to see where it led. Didn't we Blake?" In the dim light of the torch, I could see her looking towards him for confirmation of her story.

Without giving him a chance to answer, she quickly

continued, "But I tripped on a tree root and when I tried to save myself from falling, my foot kind of twisted then I couldn't get up again. It hurt so much that I couldn't put weight on it, so Blake decided to go back and get some help. Thank goodness you're here and thank goodness for Blake!"

Smiling in a coy manner, she stared directly at him and grasped his waist firmly, hanging on tightly for support.

As we slowly made our way back towards the campground and the dining area where we had hurriedly left everyone, Dad shined the torch on the ground ahead of us so that we could navigate the rutted track. There certainly were lots of tree roots that had grown across and walking along behind, I could see that it would be easy to be tripped by one if you weren't careful.

When we finally got back inside, I went to find the camp medical officer to check on Sara's ankle and as we had suspected, it was a sprain. Although, the swelling was only minor and it didn't appear to be too serious. She was then helped into a comfortable chair where she was told to raise her foot up high on some cushions that were placed on a chair in front of her. She was also given some ice packs to place on the injured area.

Quickly settling in and reveling in all the attention she was getting, she seemed quite comfortable, with no further complaints of any continuing pain. Smiling at all the faces surrounding her, she gushed appreciatively, "Thank you so much, guys! I'm really grateful for your help. And especially you, Blake! You've been so wonderful!"

"Oh, that's ok," Blake mumbled, clearly embarrassed by the praise.

"I'll come and check on you a bit later," my dad said to her, "And I'll help you make your way back to the dorms as well."

"I'll be fine thanks, Mr. Jones," Sara assured him in her sweetest voice. "Blake will help me, won't you Blake?"

Glancing awkwardly in my direction, Blake nodded in agreement and then murmured, "Yeah, sure, that's fine."

I couldn't help but notice the look of triumph in Sara's eyes as she sat back against the cushions supporting her, appearing completely satisfied with the situation at hand.

"Can you pass my microphone, please Blake?" she asked him. "We may as well get on with our rehearsal. My ankle doesn't hurt so much anymore and I can still sing, so that's all that matters."

And smiling broadly, she started on her favorite song.

The concert...

By the next afternoon, Sara's ankle had made a remarkable recovery and if I hadn't seen what I thought looked like swelling the night before, I would never have believed it had been injured at all.

Luckily for our band though, she was still able to sing and we all became more and more excited as the afternoon wore on. We'd been rehearsing for quite some time and had finally decided on the song that we would perform that evening.

There were going to be lots of acts, including some solo performances and I was surprised that Sara hadn't also wanted to perform on her own. Knowing how much she loved being the center of attention, it would have been the perfect opportunity for her to show off her voice. And I definitely had to admit, that it was a voice that was worthy of showing off. Although I begrudged her talent, I reminded myself to feel grateful that we had such a great singer amongst us.

Much to my amazement, she had actually spent the afternoon being very friendly and extra nice, particularly towards me. However, too much had gone on between us in the past and I could not bring myself to trust this sudden change of attitude. I knew Sara too well and I found it very difficult to believe that she was being genuine.

I then wondered, with a sudden rush of concern about what she was actually up to.

Perhaps the accident the night before had completely changed her outlook somehow and she had decided to become a nice person? Maybe she had hit her head and been overcome by a personality change?

Those thoughts held my attention for a fleeting moment before being whisked away.

I could hope that was the case, but deep down, I really didn't believe that such a transformation could be possible. Even though her desperate attempts to get Blake's attention had also seemed to disappear overnight, I had to trust my instincts. I decided to beware and take note of what was going on around me. But before I knew it, the time had come to head back to our dorm to get ready and I needed to focus on the concert and the song we had been practicing all afternoon. Suddenly feeling an overwhelming sense of excited anticipation, I looked forward to the night ahead.

***

A few hours later, I peered out from behind the curtain at the crowd of parents and spectators who had arrived and were seated in the audience. It seemed to be a full house and I was abruptly overcome with a bad case of nerves. But forcing myself to take a deep breath, I walked out onto the stage to introduce our act. There had been several awesome performances ahead of us including a group of three with a saxophone player. They were younger than us but were definitely tough competition.

As the rest of my band joined me on stage, I pictured in my mind, the applause I hoped we would receive at the end of our song.

We got off to a great start and I knew that we sounded pretty amazing. We had turned up the volume and when I peered into the audience, I could see the proud faces of my parents looking up at me. Even my brother, Matt had made the effort to come and I was eager to really impress them all. Then just as I was about to start my lead guitar solo, the one that everyone had been raving about and even my mentor, Andy was super impressed by, the sound from my guitar suddenly went dead.

I looked down towards my instrument and turned the knobs to adjust the volume. But nothing happened. Looking at the other guys in despair, all I got in return were blank looks and a shake of the head from Blake, indicating that he had no idea what the problem was.

Sara just shrugged her shoulders at me and returned her focus to the audience. Then, completely out of the blue, she took the microphone off its stand and strode to the front of the stage. Unexpectedly and with total confidence, she broke into a spontaneous solo performance that none of us had been at all prepared for.

Frantically, I continued to fiddle with the controls on my guitar but it was to no avail. The sound had completely died and I may as well have not been there at all!

Scanning the stage in desperation, I suddenly noticed that my guitar lead had been unplugged from the amplifier. That instantly explained why there was no sound!

"How on earth did that happen?" I wondered, completely overwhelmed with embarrassment and feeling like a fool.

When the song ended, Sara bowed proudly to the audience while I stood there feeling more awkward than ever before. Memories of our school musical where I had been totally humiliated came flooding into my mind. Then, with a gasp of realization, I looked in Sara's direction.

"Did she have anything to do with this?" I wondered wildly. "Surely, she wouldn't stoop so low as to wreck the performance of her own band?"

But the vision of her solo as she took over when I stood by helplessly, not knowing what had happened, was all too clear in my mind. And as I watched her soak up the applause that was obviously directed towards her, I felt a rage of fury surge right through me.

Of course, she denied it afterward. Of course, she knew nothing about the guitar lead that had been mysteriously unplugged from the amplifier. And of course, she was sympathetic towards me. In typical Sara fashion!

"Poor Julia!" she had exclaimed. "Your wonderful lead guitar solo that you've been working so hard on and no one could hear it. Such a shame!"

I had looked at her in disgust.

Obviously, we hadn't won the competition. The prize of recording time in a studio went to another band. But they had certainly deserved it. Their performance was incredible and in particular, the lead guitar.

When we'd packed up my gear and headed out to the car, all I could hear was Sara's voice calling out loudly for all to hear. "Goodbye, Blake. Thanks so much for looking after me! You were awesome tonight! I'll see you back at school."

And with a last look in my direction, she tossed me a wide grin and got into her mom's car ready for the trip home.

I knew that I shouldn't stoop so low, but I couldn't help myself and as soon as her back was turned, I poked out my tongue in her direction.

"Julia, what do you think you're doing?" Matt had happened to catch me in action and was shaking his head at me as if I were a real loser.

"OMG!" I thought to myself, totally embarrassed at being caught out. "Could this night possibly get any worse!!?"

Back at school...

When I met up with Millie on the bus on the first morning back to school, she listened in stunned silence as I told her about the camp. We were sitting in our usual seat at the rear, where only a few moments earlier, I had boarded the bus and we had exchanged a huge hug. After squealing crazily at the sight of each other, her first question had been, "How was music camp?"

She had known I'd been looking forward to it all summer, but since returning from the camp, we hadn't had a chance to see each other because she'd been staying with her grandparents.

Her mouth agape, she sat speechless as I told her of all the events, finishing off with the concert on the last night.

"Oh, Julia!" she exclaimed, sympathetically. "You must have been so embarrassed!"

"Yeah!" I said. "It was pretty bad!"

However, continuing on with stubborn determination, I had declared, "But I don't want to think about that anymore! This is a new school year and we have heaps to look forward to. As well, I'm focusing on us both being voted as school captains."

"Me too!" Millie eagerly replied. "It's so awesome that we were both nominated at the end of last year!"

"How cool would it be if there were two girls selected and you and I could both be the main captains together?" I cried excitedly. "I've heard of some schools doing that because there just weren't any suitable boys who had volunteered for the position."

"My mom says that girls are taking over!" I continued. "So

many more girls want to be leaders than boys, these days."

"Yeah!" Millie agreed. "And that's because we're so much better than them!'

Laughing, we high-fived each other and sat back on the seats, discussing the speeches that we had to present in front of all the upper school grades later in the week.

Both of us were feeling pretty nervous about that, but we had practiced our speeches several times throughout the holidays, so we felt prepared.

"I would love to see you and Blake voted as the captains!" Millie giggled. "That would be so good. You'd make such a great pair!" Smiling at me mischievously, she continued. "And that would really show Sara a thing or two!"

I sat there wistfully thinking about the possibility of that happening when the bus finally pulled to a stop.

As I hopped down off the steps and headed along the pathway towards our classroom, I thought once more of Blake. Deep down I knew that we were good friends and I was definitely not going to let Sara come between us. The idea of actually being his girlfriend was still something I wished for and as we climbed the stairs to our classroom, my hopes began to soar. Just as I rounded the corner to enter our room, I spotted him walking inside and I could literally feel my heart skip a beat.

Racing in after him, I realized with dismay that I was a moment too late. Sara was eagerly calling him towards her, indicating that she had saved a desk right next to hers. I could see Blake hesitate, torn between turning her down and sitting somewhere else; or agreeing to accept the offer for fear of hurting her feelings. At least that was the way I hoped he was feeling; unless he actually did want to sit next to her?

Doubt crept through my senses while at the sound of the bell, our teacher, Miss Watson, called for us all to select a desk and sit down. I had no time to consider further what might be going on in Blake's mind because the remaining desks soon began to fill with kids coming into the room. Quickly, Millie and I claimed two of the few remaining spots and I was at least grateful that I had been able to sit next to my best friend.

If only our bus had arrived at school earlier! Overcome with frustration, I shoved my books into my desk. A few moments later, I dared to sneak a glance behind me just in time to see Sara whispering in Blake's ear. And the smile that spread across his face, as he clearly became amused at whatever she had said to him, certainly didn't help to lift my spirits.

The morning dragged on and I forced myself to concentrate on the work we'd been given. I sat in my seat wondering why I had been so excited about returning to school. Work, work, and more work! And it was only our first day back. The teacher's voice droned on and on and although Millie appeared to be quite interested in what she was saying, I had failed to take in anything much at all.

During lunch break, however, everything seemed to do a sudden turnaround. We sat down in our usual spot and then to my huge surprise, Blake and his group of friends sat right beside us. Trying not to pay them too much attention, I watched in amusement out of the corner of my eye as one of the boys threw his bread crust towards Millie and it landed in her lap.

"Hey!" she called out to him and pointed in the opposite direction towards the bin. "The rubbish bin is over there!"

Then looking at me, she rolled her eyes and shook her head.

"He likes you!" I grinned, whispering quietly in her ear. But she ignored my comment and continued munching on her banana.

Just as I caught him aiming another crust at Millie, Blake unexpectedly edged himself into a vacant spot right by my side. Looking at him in surprise, I was not sure how to react. But his warm smile instantly put me at ease.

Feeling incredibly relieved to find that he was his regular self and that in fact, nothing had changed between us, I was suddenly so happy to be there right then. School had instantly become fun again and feeling ecstatic at having Blake's attention once more, I smiled happily as we chatted on about the holidays and the things that we'd both been up to since music camp.

When the bell rang for us to go back to class, Blake even suggested that we meet up sometime for a practice session to prepare for our first music lesson with Mr. Casey. Eagerly, I agreed and we decided to work out a suitable time when we were both free, possibly on a Saturday sometime soon.

After that, my mind was buzzing. We'd had several practice sessions at his place before and it was always fun. Filled with excitement, I sat back down at my desk ready for the next session but once again, found it very difficult to concentrate. This time, however, it was for a good reason, I thought to myself. Glancing behind me for the second time that day, I caught Blake's eye and the smile he gave me made my heart melt with joy.

Sara, who had disappeared during the lunch break for some reason, seemed to have become aware of the glances between Blake and myself and I watched her trying to get his attention once more.

"Just stay positive, Julia!" I said quietly to myself as I attempted to get started on the work that Miss Watson had put on the board. "Focus on what you want to happen!"

"Did you say something?" Millie leaned over and whispered in my ear.

"Oh, it's ok," I replied, grinning widely. "I was just talking to myself!"

With a shake of her head, she rolled her eyes and gave me a

little poke with her elbow, at the same time laughing in amusement.

"Anything to do with Blake Jansen?" she asked.

"Maybe!" I replied, grinning widely. And with a huge sigh, I put my head down to do some work, but all I could manage was to scrawl the words, 'Blake and Julia' over and over on my notepad.

Goal Setting...

The day of the big assembly finally came and after a great week at school hanging out with Millie, Blake and several other friends (and managing to ignore Sara), we suddenly found ourselves sitting in our class groups in the school hall. We were dressed in our school uniforms which were saved for special occasions such as this, and several of us were feeling very anxious. The new school captains were going to be announced that morning and in particular, Millie and I were desperately hoping that we'd been chosen.

We had to present our speeches the week before and we had both been pretty nervous. Although we practiced heaps during the holidays and felt prepared, it was still a nerve-wracking thing to do.

But I'd taken advice from my mom and ensured I made lots of eye contact with the audience, all the while focusing on speaking clearly and sounding confident.

There was always a girl and a boy captain selected and a girl and a boy vice-captain as well. I had my heart set on being captain and Millie was hoping to become sports captain. She's pretty sporty and I was sure that she'd be great in that role.

Being school captain was something I had thought about for a long time. Even though I used to be really shy, I always loved watching the captains on stage at assembly and on special occasions when they were given the opportunity to represent our school. I thought it would be such a cool thing to do and although I had never pictured myself having enough courage to take on such a role, I've gradually become more confident and so decided to give it a go. I'm sure being captain will help to increase my confidence further still and I know this will be a huge advantage in the future.

During the summer holidays, I did something to try to help myself achieve this goal. I made a dream board which is now on the wall of my bedroom, right next to my bed. I spent almost an entire day, drawing and cutting out magazine pictures of things that I would love to have and also of things that I would like to become.

Then I pinned them onto a large corkboard that my mom agreed to buy for me from one of the local craft shops. I decorated it with a pretty border and filled it with lots of really cool pictures that I can look at every day and focus on. I also wrote some of my goals out and attached those as well.

One of them says…

I am now school captain and I'm so happy, I am over the moon! ☺

This was a technique that I learned in the book of dreams that I read last year. By writing my goals down as if I have already achieved them, will help to make them actually happen.

If I wrote…"I am *going* to be school captain *next year*," then it will always be in the future and I would never achieve that goal as it will always be... "*next year*."

Whereas, stating it as if it's already happened, helps me to believe that it's possible. This is much more effective and helps to make it come true.

Another picture that I've added to my dream board is of a beautiful chestnut horse. Ever since I was a little girl, I've always wanted a horse of my own and over the years, I've spent endless amounts of time dreaming about owning one.

Mom told me not to be so silly and get my hopes up over things that will probably never eventuate. But I decided to ignore her advice and wrote that goal down on paper anyway. Then I pinned it directly beneath the picture of my dream pony. I know that if you stay positive and really focus on things, miracles definitely can happen. It's worth trying anyway. And I love dreaming about horses, so I have nothing to lose. When I'm not dreaming about Blake that is! ☺

The announcement...

It was just then that the microphone crackled again and I was shaken out of my little daydream by the reality that was going on around me. They were announcing the sports captains first and I crossed my fingers that Millie's name would be the one to be called.

First, Reece Wilson was announced as the new boys' sports captain and he proudly walked up the steps of the stage to accept his certificate.

Then it was time for the girls' name to be announced. Crossing my fingers tightly, I prayed that it would be Millie's.

When her name was in fact called out, I could not contain my excitement. "Yessss!" I squealed and gave her a quick hug.

I felt really happy for her as she headed up onto the stage. I caught her eye and gave her a beaming smile which she excitedly acknowledged with a big smile of her own.

Shaking hands with Mrs. Harding, our school principal, Millie accepted her certificate and stood next to Reece. Everyone was then told that the badges for each captain would be engraved with their names and handed out during assembly the following week. I was so thrilled for Millie and cheered once more.

Then, over the microphone were the words, "Next, we will announce the school captains."

I could feel butterflies in my stomach and I gripped hold of the edge of the chair I was sitting on as I sat anxiously waiting for Mrs. Harding to say the names.

"The boys' captain for this year is Blake Jansen." My

stomach took a crazy dive as I pictured the two of us up on stage together. That really would be a 'dream come true.'

The noise in the assembly hall erupted as everyone cheered Blake on. He was very popular and obviously, the boy who all the kids had been hoping would be elected. I clapped wildly, feeling so happy for him to have been given that honor.

Another boy called, Mitch Benson was elected as the boys' vice-captain and as he walked onto the stage, the applause and cheering erupted once more.

Then as I sat there, fearfully waiting for the girls' names to be announced, Mrs. Harding was suddenly called away from the microphone and handed another piece of paper. The deputy principal was urgently whispering something in her ear and it was clear that they were discussing the contents of the paper in front of them.

Being kept in complete suspense like that caused a sick feeling in the pit of my stomach. "What's going on? Why can't they just make the announcement?" The apprehension that was flooding through me was almost too much to bear.

The atmosphere in the hall became quite tense and uncomfortable and I felt sorry for my friends standing on the stage, as they had no idea what was going on.

Then all of a sudden and out of nowhere, I felt my skin crawl. It was an eerie sensation but also one I recalled feeling a few times before. I knew that I was nervous but it didn't explain the prickly numbness I had been overcome with. For some reason, I felt compelled to look behind me. It was as if I had been forced to turn around, and staring directly at me with eyes like daggers, was Sara Hamilton.

Up until that moment, I had managed to clear her from my

mind. I knew that she was also desperate to be the girls' captain and I'd even heard about her bribing the other kids to vote for her. Not that she needed it, I thought to myself, as she was popular enough without having to stoop to that level.

Since the music camp and the first day back at school, I had been desperately trying to keep negative thoughts at bay, which was why I refused to focus on Sara's determination to be voted as captain this year. An image of her standing on the stage next to Blake flashed through my mind, but I quickly shook it away.

"NO!" I reminded myself. "Stay positive, Julia! You can do this!"

It was just then that the microphone crackled once more. "I'm very sorry for the delay," apologized Mrs. Harding, "But after double checking, it appears that we had the names of the girls' captains incorrectly recorded. Thank goodness for our thorough office staff, who noticed the error." She gave a small laugh but no one acknowledged it. I mean how could she be laughing at a time like this anyway?

"The votes for the position of girls' captain were extremely close this year," she continued. "In fact, there was only one vote between these two girls."

"OMG!" I heard someone nearby mumble just a little too loudly. "Can you please just tell us who it is?"

"Congratulations to Sara Hamilton." As the words were uttered I could feel my stomach drop with despair. It was like a huge weight had taken hold and pushed it all the way to the ground.

But after a slight pause to clear her throat, Mrs. Harding continued, "Sara, you have been elected vice-captain this year and Julia Jones, is our new girl's captain. Congratulations to both of you!"

"Oh my gosh! Oh my gosh!" I could hear the words tumbling from my mouth in shocked surprise. Riveted to the spot, I stood transfixed with excitement. The whole scene seemed surreal, almost as if I were watching myself in a movie.

Taking charge of my senses, I edged along the row of seats towards the aisle. Overwhelmed with excitement, I made my way onto the stage where the others were already assembled. Millie's huge smile was proof of how happy she was for me and I smiled widely in return. Then, looking towards Blake, I could see his look of obvious delight at the outcome we had all been waiting to hear and this just added to the pleasure I was feeling. Not even the glaring stare from Sara as she walked along the stage to stand next to Mitch, could spoil that moment.

School captain! I had been elected school captain!!

I had achieved my goal and I'm sure that I was the happiest person in that room right then.

I stood with the others as the audience, which included all the parents of our grade, applauded us. It was probably one of the most special occasions I have ever experienced and one I'll always remember.

As soon as we were handed our certificates and the assembly was drawn to a close, I gave Blake a big high-five then raced over to Millie to exchange a warm hug.

"Congratulations, guys!" I said to them both. "We did it!"

Deciding that I should set an example, I walked over to Sara and held out my hand in congratulations. Her first reaction was to simply stare at me in disgust, but knowing that we were being watched by teachers and parents who were standing nearby, forced her to raise her hand to mine. "Congratulations, Sara!" I said, with total confidence and then turned and headed off the stage alongside Millie.

Proudly, we joined our parents for the special morning tea

that had been prepared for the new captains and their moms and dads.

A photographer was there to take our photos, and Blake and I, posing for our first ever photo in our role as school captains, smiled for the camera.

Copies were printed and handed out to each of us later that day. Amongst them was one that I really loved and it instantly became my new favorite. I packed it carefully inside a book where it wouldn't get crushed and decided that I would add it to my dream board when I got home.

I thought surely there was no harm in that, and I couldn't wait to get off the bus that afternoon so I could race up to my room. I knew that photo would make my dream board look better than ever!

Celebrations...

My parents took me out for dinner that night, to my favorite Italian restaurant. They were so proud and couldn't help but announce to everyone they came across that I'd been elected school captain. People seemed to be very impressed with that. I'd had no idea that it would be such a big deal to everyone and I was glad that I had made the effort to go ahead and apply for the position.

As I sat munching on my favorite pizza, I thought about the weekend ahead. Blake had invited me over to his house the next afternoon so that we could do some practice on the drums and guitar. We were both keen to amaze Mr. Casey in our first lesson, which he had arranged for the following week. I was certainly looking forward to that but what I was looking forward to most was the afternoon that lay ahead. Thoughts of Blake made me smile with anticipation.

"What are you grinning about?" my brother, Matt asked me curiously.

"Oh, I'm just really enjoying this pizza," I replied innocently.

There was no way I was going to tell him what I was really thinking. That would just be too embarrassing. And besides, all Matt wanted to talk about was basketball, motorbikes, and girls.

He actually liked one of the girls in his class. He didn't know that I knew, but his friend, Billy told me when he was over one afternoon.

"Did you know that Matt has a huge crush on Molly Ringwood?" he asked me as we sat watching a movie on TV.

Matt had disappeared into the kitchen to get some food and was out of earshot. I had no idea why Billy decided to tell me that, but I teased Matt about it later, after Billy had left.

Previously, he'd been going out with a girl called Lily Thompson but they'd broken up for some reason. He hadn't wanted to talk about it at the time and I had known he was quite upset. Although he did seem to get over it fairly quickly and maybe that was because Molly had appeared on the scene.

"Do you know a girl called Molly Ringwood, Matt?" I asked him, pretending that I had heard her name somewhere and I just wondered who she was.

It was so funny to see his face turn bright red, just at the mention of her name. It was clearly obvious that what Billy had said was true, but I didn't comment any further except to say, "I've heard that she goes to your school and she's really pretty!"

He mumbled a reply that didn't make much sense. He was embarrassed to even talk about her. It cracked me up inside though. I love teasing him and making him squirm like that. He certainly embarrasses me often enough, so I always take advantage if I get an opportunity.

Mom says he's going through a stage. Although I must admit, after being grounded for two weeks, he's definitely improved his attitude. And at least he now does his share of the chores around the house, rather than leaving everything to me.

"Brothers!" I thought to myself, as I reached for another piece of pizza, all the while watching Matt gulp down his fifth slice.

Lately, he has actually been less annoying and sometimes he's even really nice. At times, he asks for my advice on things, like what T-shirt he should wear or which jeans look best. He never used to care about stuff like that, but now he really takes his time getting ready to go just about anywhere. The only problem is that he now spends even longer than before in the bathroom, so I have to make sure I get up earlier in the mornings, so I can use it before him. Otherwise, I'd never be on time for the bus.

Secretly, I think that my brother is pretty cool. Although, I'd never tell him that!

Millie commented recently that she thought he was good looking. I couldn't believe it when she said that.

Could my brother Matt, actually be good looking?

I'm still not sure about that but sometimes, I must admit, I do quite enjoy having him for my brother; when he's not annoying me that is!

The weekend…

Saturday afternoon could not come quickly enough and as I jumped out of the car and reached across the back seat for my guitar, I thanked my dad for giving me a lift then gave him a quick kiss goodbye.

"I'll be back at 5:30 to pick you up!" he reminded me just before he drove off. Acknowledging him with a wave, I raced down the pathway towards the music studio that was situated at the back of the garage, and from where I could hear Blake banging away on his drums.

He was so focused on what he was playing that he didn't see me enter and I sneaked up behind him, gently placing my hands over his eyes.

"Guess who?" I asked teasingly, realizing that he'd obviously know the answer but I was unable to resist the temptation.

"Um…Meg Nolan?" he questioned in an attempt at a convincingly sincere tone. Meg was one of the really popular girls in our class and also one of Sara's friends.

"No!" I replied indignantly, resisting the urge to giggle. "Guess again!"

"Would it happen to be a really good guitarist who has now become school captain and her name is Julia Jones?"

Laughing, I removed my hands and sat down on the chair in front of him. The sweet smile he gave me, created that familiar fuzzy feeling in my stomach; the one that I'd been experiencing a lot lately, in particular when I was around Blake. And I smiled shyly in return.

An awkward kind of silence erupted between us and seemed to last for several seconds. All we seemed capable of doing was to stare at each other. To break the weirdness, I began babbling on with ideas for songs that we could practice.

"We really need to impress Mr. Casey in our lesson next week, so let's get started," I suggested, trying to overcome the anxious sensation in the pit of my stomach.

"Ok," he replied with a grin. And I was very grateful when he grabbed his drumsticks and started banging away on his drums.

Thankfully, we then became engrossed in our music and the following two hours were spent in constant rehearsal mode. We were so focused that we had no idea how quickly the time passed by.

When we finally stopped for a break, Blake suggested that we go inside for a drink and a snack. His mom had made some chocolate brownies and I could smell the delicious aroma wafting from the kitchen.

She handed us a plate and we took it outside to their back deck where we sat down to eat. Then, laughing comfortably, we chatted about the assembly the day before and how nervous we had both been, especially when Mrs. Harding had mixed up the names of the captains.

As I munched quietly on my brownie, Blake suddenly and quite unexpectedly grabbed my hand and pulled me to my feet. "Come down to the back garden!" he exclaimed. "There's something that I want to show you."

Clutching my hand tightly, he led me along a pebbled pathway towards the winding creek that bordered the back of the property. Blake's family was very lucky as their house was built on an extremely large block of land that backed onto some dense bush and this ran along the edge of the creek. Although they lived on a suburban street, once out in the back garden it was totally private and very pretty.

Suddenly Blake slowed his pace and began to tread softly as he approached a grassy patch hidden by tall reeds and shrubs. Putting a finger to his lips he indicated that we needed to be very quiet. It was a section that was well camouflaged and without knowing exactly where to look, it would have been very easy to miss.

He bent down on his knees and I peered over his shoulder, where I could see hidden amongst the grass, a kind of nest from which I could hear a distinct but very soft clucking sound; then to my huge delight, a pair of little black eyes surrounded by yellow fluff, peered up at me. With sudden recognition, I realized that there were six little ducklings sitting quietly next to their mother. She was a tawny brown color that blended with her surroundings; however, the bright yellow of the ducklings' fur glistened boldly in the afternoon sun.

"Oooh!" I gasped. "They're the cutest things I've ever seen!"

"Do you want to hold one?" Blake asked, delighted by my reaction. "I found them this morning when I was wandering around down here. The mother doesn't mind too much, as long as you stay close."

"I'd love to!" I exclaimed and as he passed me the tiny bundle of yellow downy fur, the smile on my face was of pure enchantment.

"They are so beautiful," I whispered, gently stroking the little duckling's tiny head and back. A few moments later, I returned the precious little creature to its nest. The mother had become slightly agitated, so I decided not to disturb them further.

Then without warning, she got to her feet and waddled down towards the water, quacking as she went. The tiny babies spontaneously followed along behind her. Watching them walk in a line, one after the other was a fascinating and beautiful sight and I laughed at the pure joy of it all.

As we observed them quietly, we could see that the smallest duckling which was desperately attempting to keep up was almost left behind. So Blake decided to give it a helping hand and gently carried the little fellow to the water's edge. Then, with no hesitation whatsoever, the whole family hit the water and the little ones instantly began swimming around in circles alongside their mother, obviously overjoyed at being able to do what ducks do best.

We looked on in absolute awe and I felt so privileged to witness the beautiful spectacle of nature in our midst. Then suddenly, I felt a slight touch on my hand. I looked down enthralled, as Blake's fingers curled gently around mine and as I gazed upwards, our eyes met.

"Julia," he said, softly. "I've wanted to ask you something for quite a while now."

"Really?" I asked, my stomach in complete knots as I stood there staring towards him.

"Do you want to go out with me? I mean, you know…go out with me?" He was stumbling over his words, seemingly unsure of what my response was going to be.

But the reply tumbled automatically from my lips, "Yes, Blake. I would!"

The beaming grin that spread across his face right then was so contagious that I couldn't help but do the same. And as he wrapped his arms around me in a huge embrace, I thought my heart would burst with joy.

Then, sitting side by side, we sat to watch the wonder of the beautiful little creatures in front of us. It was like a miracle, I thought, as they swam along completely at ease behind their mother.

But that wasn't the only miracle that had happened that day. And the wonder of that thought floated gently through my mind as I rested my head on Blake's shoulder.

Sighing with total contentment, I realized that nothing else mattered right then except the magic of that very moment.

And I wished it could go on forever!

Being grateful...

Lying in bed that night, I thought about the afternoon I had shared with Blake. I almost had to pinch myself to be sure that it hadn't simply been a dream that I'd just woken up from. But I knew deep down in my heart that it was real. I'd had the biggest crush on Blake for so long and now he was actually my boyfriend. My first boyfriend! I giggled to myself in awe of what had come about.

Then I thought about my phone call to Millie as soon as I had walked in the door. Of course, I couldn't wait to tell her and I'd come upstairs to the privacy of my room so that no one else could hear my conversation. There was no way I wanted Matt to know, that was for sure. He would just tease me about it.

"Julia's got a boyfriend! Julia's got a boyfriend!" I could just hear him now!

As much as his attitude towards me had improved lately, he still did stupid stuff at times. Plus, I wasn't sure how my parents would react. Mom was always worried about my schoolwork and I know she'd think my grades would be affected. So I decided to just keep it between Millie and myself.

As I'd expected, she had squealed with surprise on the phone, when I told her all about my afternoon. Millie had wanted to hear all the details and I'd started at the very beginning from when my dad had dropped me off, right up to the moment when Blake held my hand and finally asked me to go out with him.

Thinking about that moment took my breath away and I smiled with excitement.

There were a few other girls and boys in our class who were

already going out together and I also knew that Millie really liked Blake's friend, Jack. Ever since he joined our dance troupe for the musical last year, I could tell that she had a crush on him. But she would never admit it to me.

At one stage, she was obsessed with Harry Robinson. Luckily, she eventually found out what a loser he was though. And he's actually become even worse this year! He literally thinks he's better than anyone else in the entire school and I can't believe that I actually liked him myself for a brief time. It just goes to show that you really can't judge a book by its cover. I've decided I will definitely take time to get to know people before judging them in future!

Anyway, after sharing my news with Millie on the phone, I immediately began to devise a plan to get her and Jack together. If that happened, then maybe we could all hang out at school and on weekends. That would be so cool!

As I rolled over in bed, I could see that the bright moonlight shining through my window had illuminated my dream board and in particular, the photo with Blake's smiling face caught my eye. Once more I thought about the wonderful hug he had given me that afternoon. I had barely been able to stop smiling ever since.

After admiring the pictures that were aglow on my wall, my attention was then drawn towards the list of goals I had written. The one about becoming school captain seemed to jump out at me. While reading the words, I was overcome with a dawning realization. Several of my dreams had actually become a reality. Not just one of them, but several!

With a rush of excitement, I considered the techniques I had used to make this happen.

Apart from attaching pictures and handwritten goals to my dream board so I could look at the images and read the words each day, I knew the other things that I did were equally important. I also had to create a picture in my mind of the things I wanted to happen.

There have been many times when I've pictured myself wearing a school captain's badge with my name on it. I was overcome with excitement as I visualized the scene where I walked up onto the stage after my name was announced. I remembered laying on my bed and feeling goosebumps. It was almost like watching a movie in my head, but it had seemed so real.

One day, as I lay there visualizing my goals and dreams, Matt barged into my room and started shaking me. "What are you doing, Julia?" he had bellowed in my ear. "You've got a huge smile on your face. Are you sleeping or are you daydreaming again?"

Feeling so annoyed at the interruption, I yelled at him to get out. I didn't admit to him, what I had actually been doing. He would have just laughed at me and said I was weird.

But I really didn't care what he thought. If it helped me to make wonderful things happen in my life, then I was going to do it, whether he laughed at me or not!

Making miracles happen was so incredible and I felt in awe of what I was capable of if I set my mind to it.

I felt so grateful right then. I was always sure to be thankful for everything I had and I knew that would allow even more things to come into my life for me to be grateful for. Practicing gratitude was probably the most important part.

That was actually another thing Matt made fun of recently when he overheard me saying, "Thank you!" out loud. He had asked me who I was talking to but when he realized that I was talking to myself, he'd yelped, "I knew you were crazy!" and had rolled around on the floor in hysterics. "Ha! Ha! Ha! My sister really is a weirdo!"

I was pretty embarrassed. I certainly hadn't meant to talk out loud. But I was so absorbed in my thoughts that I hadn't even realized I was actually speaking.

I just rolled my eyes at him and told him he should try being grateful himself for once, rather than always expecting stuff and complaining when he didn't get what he wanted.

"How can you ever expect to have more things in your life when you're not even grateful for what you already have?" I looked at him questioningly, but he just ignored me and continued on with the stupid game he'd been playing.

I might even make that my mission, I decided. I would find a time when he was not on his X-box or the computer and try to explain how it all worked. It would be great to see him changing his outlook.

I knew it would take some effort. But maybe I should mention Molly Ringwood? That might convince him to listen to me!

It was worth a try anyway! ☺

Plans for the term...

I felt a little nervous about arriving at school on Monday morning and as I entered the classroom, I looked shyly in Blake's direction. He gave me one of his cheeky grins and waved. Sitting down at my desk, I could not wipe the beaming smile from my face. Millie, who had acknowledged what was going on, just poked me with her elbow and laughed.

I was so excited for break time so that Blake and I could hang out together. I'd spent Sunday afternoon doing some baking and had packed some extra chocolate muffins in my lunch box. Grinning with anticipation, I pictured the smile on his face as I handed him one.

Forcing myself to concentrate on the Math that had been put on the board for us to complete, I put my head down and got on with my work until finally, the clang of the lunch bell signaled the end of the morning session.

Impatiently, everyone leaped from their seats, grabbed their lunch boxes from their bags, and headed down the stairs. Millie and I sat with our usual group in our usual spot and I waited eagerly for Blake to join us. Meanwhile, I offered Millie one of the chocolate muffins. Knowing how much she loves them, I always pack extra and her grateful reaction is always worth the effort.

It made me think once more of how showing your gratitude can bring more of what you're grateful for into your life. It certainly works that way for Millie with my muffins! She always says the biggest thank you and enjoys them so much, that sometimes I even go to the trouble of baking them just for her. And that's simply because she's always so thankful. I guess I'll have to come up with a new favorite recipe soon though before she becomes bored with the same old flavor.

Although she enjoys these ones so much, she's convinced that they'll always be her favorite.

Glancing around, I hoped to see Blake heading towards us, but there seemed to be no sign of him. As I sat dejectedly munching on my food, I listened half-heartedly while everyone else chatted about their weekend and the things that they had been up to. Then, just as our break time was drawing to an end, I caught sight of him coming around a corner. Much to my surprise, however, Sara was right behind him, chatting animatedly about something that obviously held the attention of both of them. They certainly appeared to be absorbed in the conversation they were having.

Blake's group of friends was sitting in the same area as us and I waited for him to join them but he kept on walking towards the office, Sara right by his side.

My first thought had been one of suspicion. This is something I find hard to avoid when Sara becomes involved with any of us. But I forced all negative ideas from my mind as I remembered the wonderful afternoon that I had shared with Blake just two days earlier.

When the bell rang a little while later, I looked down at the uneaten muffin that I had saved for Blake, still sitting wrapped in paper inside my lunch box. As I closed the lid, I decided that I would just give it to him at lunchtime.

When we returned to our classroom, Millie and I gathered the things we would need for the computer lab, which our class was scheduled for right then, and followed the others along the walkway.

As soon as the door to the computer room was opened, everyone scrambled frantically in their usual manner, hoping to secure a computer next to one of their friends. It was the regular scenario whenever we had computer lab time but Miss Watson was not used to this sort of behavior and a couple of rowdy boys were told to separate.

Just as we started on the research task we'd been instructed to complete with a partner, Blake and Sara rushed into the room.

"Sorry we're late, Miss Watson!" Sara said breathlessly. "Mr. Thompson asked us to deliver a message to all the upper school teachers. Here it is," She said, passing her a handwritten note.

"Oh, ok, thanks, Sara," replied Miss Watson as she scanned the message and then proceeded to read it to us.

"Listen up, guys!" she said. "There's a regional track tournament coming up in about three weeks' time and Mr. Thompson would like to enter a girls' and a boys' running team. He has requested that anyone who is interested in trying out should go straight to his office when the bell rings for the lunch break. He will hand out notes and explain all the details then."

The room was instantly abuzz with excitement as everyone began discussing the upcoming event. There were a number of very good athletes in our grade and it was obvious that there would be a great deal of interest. I looked towards Millie, knowing for sure that she would want to participate. She was a very good runner and I was convinced that she'd be a definite candidate.

"You should try out too," she said to me, reading my mind. "It would be so much fun if we both made the team."

"I'd love to!" I told her, "But I'm not a great runner like you!"

"Julia Jones!" she exclaimed mockingly. "What are those words that just came out of your mouth? Where is the positive attitude that you're always talking to me about? Shame on you!"

As her laughter subsided, she took on a serious expression. "I'm not joking, Julia. You should at least give it a go!"

It only took a moment for me to consider what she had said.

"Do you know what?" I replied firmly. "You're absolutely right!"

And as an afterthought, I added, "And Millie! Thanks for reminding me!" I gave her a wink and a grateful grin. Looking at my friend then, I felt really impressed. She had actually taken on board some of the stuff I'd been saying to her about maintaining a positive attitude. And now she was helping to keep me on track!

"The words that you speak are just as important as the thoughts in your mind, Millie," is what I had said to her only recently. "Keep your words and thoughts positive, because whatever you think about and talk about is what will come into your life!"

At the time, I'd thought she had pretty much ignored my rambling. But obviously, she had really taken it in.

"What a team we are," I thought to myself as I smiled at her once more.

"OK, Millie!" I said out loud. "Let's do it! We'll go straight to Mr. Thompson at lunchtime and nominate ourselves. I can picture us both on that running team. We're going to kill it!"

"Hmphh! I wouldn't be so sure if I were you. Places are limited and only the best runners will be included. So be prepared to be disappointed!" Sara's mocking tone interrupted us as she strutted past, Blake shuffling along behind her.

"Here we go Blake!' she said loudly, making sure that we heard her. "Miss Watson said that we'll have to pair up for this assignment, so you can have this computer right next to mine." And she patted the seat, beckoning him to sit beside her.

Looking uneasily at me, I could see his face turning red with embarrassment as he searched for an alternative spot. Unfortunately…the last available computer was the one that Sara had indicated. And besides that, there was no one else for him to work with.

Smiling with triumph, Sara glanced my way once more before whispering something in Blake's ear and then, laughing mischievously, she waited for her computer to start up.

Doing my best to ignore her, I focused on the task sheet and punched the keys on the keyboard as I searched for the information I needed.

But out of the corner of my eye, I could see Sara enjoying herself immensely while she worked with Blake on the history assignment we'd been given.

Well, that's what they were supposed to be working on but gauging by the smile on her face, I wasn't too sure. And Blake seemed to be enjoying himself just as much as Sara.

Trying to focus on the computer screen in front of me, I forced myself not to worry about it and before long I was absorbed in the task. I'm not sure how much Sara and Blake got done though!

The sign on...

"Ok, guys," Mr. Thompson announced, to all the kids sitting on the floor outside his office. "As you've already been told, I'd like to enter a girls' team and a boys' team for the regional track event that is coming up in three weeks' time. Now, I can only take 4 girls and 4 boys plus 2 reserves for each team. But the problem is that there are several great runners amongst you!"

We all looked at him expectantly and wondered how he was going to choose. Everyone was pretty excited about this event and there had already been some speculation about who would be chosen.

We listened avidly as he continued. "So I've decided that the fairest way is for you to sign up for training sessions and the final teams will be selected based on not only your running ability but also the level of commitment that's displayed during the training period."

"If you feel that you can commit to training every morning before school, then by all means, you're welcome to try out. But anyone who misses more than two sessions without a valid excuse will be dropped from the squad."

"But I can't come on Thursdays and Fridays because I have tennis lessons," complained a girl sitting at the back of the group.

"And I have to catch the bus to school, so I can't make it in the mornings," called a boy from my class.

"I realize that this schedule won't suit everyone," Mr. Thompson replied. "But we have limited time to prepare and I only want kids involved who are able to commit. So, if you're serious about this, add your name to the list, take a permission note home for your parents to sign and I'll see you here at 8 am tomorrow morning."

My first thought was that this was just not possible for me. It would mean that I'd have to catch the really early bus and I already struggled with catching my regular bus as it was. But then I caught a glimpse of Sara, giggling in Blake's ear as she added her name to the sheet being passed around. We made eye contact and she then whispered something more to Blake before making a show of whispering in his ear once again.

Millie, who had witnessed her blatant flirting, suddenly said to me very quietly, "Just ignore her, Julia! Blake mentioned to Jimmy that you guys are going out together. Now I think somehow, Sara's found out and she's probably trying to make you jealous!"

Hearing that just made me more determined, "If it means I have to get up extra early for the next three weeks, then that's the way it is!" I said to Millie. "Because I'm going to do everything I can to be on that team!"

Glancing at Sara once more, I added firmly, "It's time to be more assertive! There's no way I'm going to let her affect me the way she has in the past!"

Drawing in a deep breath, I flicked my hair out of my eyes, threw my shoulders back and strode confidently past her. All the while, she sat waiting and watching my every move.

"Hey, Julia!" Blake said, smiling happily, completely unaware of what was going on between Sara and I. "I've been waiting all day to hang out with you! Let's go and get some lunch."

And without another look back, I signed the sheet, handed it to Mr. Thompson then walked alongside Blake and Millie to the lunch area. And all the while, I could almost feel the heat of Sara's eyes burning into my back as she stared after us in disgust.

Managing to push all thoughts of Sara from my mind, I decided to focus on the two most special people in my life right then, remembering that you get what you focus on. And spending time with Millie and Blake was high on my priority list. As I made that decision, I could feel the tension drain out of me and we spent the lunch break chatting about the tournament and how much fun it was going to be for us all to be on the team together.

Then out of the blue and catching me by complete surprise, Blake suddenly grabbed hold of my hand. He looked towards me as if to ensure that I was ok with his sudden gesture. I glanced around shyly, a bit uncomfortable about holding hands at school. But then I saw Millie's discreet wink and all concern melted away.

There is nothing wrong with holding hands is there?

After all, we are girlfriend and boyfriend! ☺

Visions of winning…

Sitting on the early bus the next morning, I glanced out the window as I considered the events of the previous afternoon. As soon as I'd arrived home, I raced upstairs to my room and pulled out a piece of paper. On it I had written, the following…

"I am now on the school running team, competing in the regional event and I have won my race."

I then attached my latest goal to my dream board along with a picture that I'd drawn of myself in running gear. I had a huge smile on my face and a winner's trophy in my hand. Knowing that it was a very large goal, I leaned back on my bed and contemplated the display I had just put together, trying to keep the doubt from creeping into my thoughts. But with a sudden resolve, I remembered that I needed to dream big and as long as I worked towards my goal, then it was definitely possible for me to achieve it.

After eating dinner and helping to clean up the kitchen, I had decided to have an early night's sleep. I was determined more than ever I would be on that team but to do that, I was aware of the amount of work ahead of me. However, I knew that by applying effort, along with a positive attitude and belief in my abilities, anything was possible. I then closed my eyes and pictured myself racing down the track, my arms in the air in victory as I crossed the finish line ahead of the other competitors.

Covered in goose bumps at the thrill of the vision I had created in my mind, I laughed out loud, feeling happy and confident. And then, out of the blue, Blake's handsome face flashed into my thoughts. As I fell into a blissful sleep, dreams of Blake and running tracks and blue ribbons all rolled into one.

I think the smile was still on my face when my alarm went off in the morning and I eagerly leapt out of bed, excited about the day ahead.

When my bus pulled up at the school gates, I raced towards the oval, where we'd been told to meet and I was greeted along the way by Millie, who had just been dropped off at school by her mom.

Both of us dressed in training gear, we joined the group that was waiting for Mr. Thompson to arrive and soon after, Blake's smiling face also appeared, trailed closely behind by Sara, who I chose to ignore. I knew that she would soon give up, if she saw she was having no effect on me.

Then, after doing our warm-up exercises, the girls all took off around the track, jogging at a steady pace. Surprising myself, I found that I was able to actually keep up with some of them and in particular, a girl called Amy Duncan, who is a very good runner. My hopes soared! With regular and consistent training, I could already see my goal becoming a reality.

The list...

The days passed by quickly with the early morning starts all blending into one. It felt as though each morning when my alarm went off, I had only just fallen asleep, but my determination to be chosen for the running team motivated me to persist.

Meanwhile, Blake and I both blitzed our first music session with Mr. Casey, who was extremely impressed with the level we had reached. Beaming with pride, we had high-fived each other, although we knew that it was the effort we'd been putting in that had enabled us to get to that stage. We then decided to arrange another practice session at his house.

I sat at my desk trying to focus on schoolwork but the buzz of excitement at spending another Saturday afternoon with Blake had prevented me from getting anything done. Suddenly my chain of thought was interrupted by the crackle of the school intercom.

"This is a message for everyone in the regional running squad." It was Mr. Thompson speaking and I sat up to take notice. "I will post the details of the final selection on the noticeboard outside my office this afternoon. Please check the list and if you have made the team, make sure you're at training at 8am in the morning."

I glanced at Millie. "That's us!" I said confidently, completely sure that we had been chosen. And I pictured once more, the vision of myself being the first to cross the finish line in the final race of the tournament.

Looking in Blake's direction, I caught his beautiful smile as well as his thumbs up sign. This was followed by a scornful shake of the head from Sara, her blue eyes staring at me as if to say, "There's no way you'll be in that team, Julia!"

Ignoring her however, I returned my attention to the front of the room and attempted to concentrate on the Geography activity I'd been working on.

The afternoon session seemed to drag by and when the bell finally sounded, we raced to pack up and get out the door, keen to be the first to see the list on Mr. Thompson's noticeboard.

Laughing as we ran, Blake grabbed hold of my hand so that I could keep pace with him. "Come on, Millie!" I called. "If you're going to be on the running team, you need to be able to run faster than that!" And I reached for her hand, to drag her along with us.

There was already a small crowd milling around the board by the time we finally reached it and I could hear shrieks of joy as kids realized they had made the team.

"Not fair!" sighed a boy from a different class to ours as he pushed through the throng, the disappointment evident on his face after finding out that he hadn't been selected.

Hurriedly scanning the list, I spotted Blake's name and could see that he'd been chosen as one of the top four boys. Filled with excitement, I moved my eyes to the list of girls' names. Millie's was on top and I squealed loudly. The following names were Amy Mitchell, Sara Hamilton, Becky Whitfield and Jodie Milford as a reserve.

"That can't be right!" I thought to myself as I quickly scanned the list once more.

I could feel my stomach drop. My name was not there. But how could it not be there? My head was spinning. It didn't make any sense to me and I was overcome with shock and despair. This wasn't meant to happen!

Turning around slowly, the look of triumph in Sara's eyes as she stared straight into mine, filled me with embarrassment and torment.

I'd been so sure! And I had told everybody I would be on that team. Millie, Blake and I were supposed to be celebrating right now, but Sara had won out instead.

"Yessss!!!!" she yelled loudly, ensuring I was taking in her look of victory. "Blake! Millie! We made it!!! We're on the team!"

"It's going to be so cool!!!!" she continued.

Her enthusiasm sickened me to the core.

"Don't cry, Julia! Whatever you do, don't cry!" The words raced through my head as I desperately tried to put on a brave front.

I forced myself to speak. "Congratulations, guys!"

I was genuinely happy for Millie and Blake but the disappointment about not making the team myself was too much to bear. So I quickly mumbled, "Sorry, but I've got to run or I'll miss my bus. I'll see you tomorrow."

And with that, I took off in the direction of the bus stop, eternally grateful that I had an excuse to escape the looks of sympathy from my friends, not to mention Sara's moment of glory.

Racing to the back where I claimed a seat next to the window, I could feel the tears in my eyes begin to fall. As I miserably wiped them away, I faced towards the window in order to avoid looks from the kids around me. I was unable to stop the flow of tears and I desperately wanted to get home to the security and safety of my bedroom.

The instant the bus pulled up at my stop, I was out the door, head bowed low and hidden from view. Approaching our front gate, I was totally dismayed to see it swing abruptly open. The sight of my brother, Matt was not one that I welcomed at all.

"What's wrong?" he asked, genuine concern showing on his face at the sight of my puffy red eyes and tear-stained cheeks.

"Leave me alone!" I replied angrily and barged straight past him.

I didn't want to see or speak to anyone right then and I bolted up the stairs, taking them two at a time. Then, rushing into my room, I slammed the door shut behind me.

Two choices...

Throwing myself onto my bed, I grabbed hold of my teddy and burst into tears.

"It's not fair!" I sobbed as I thumped my fist into the pillow.

Sobbing even louder, I yelled again, "It's not fair!!!!!!!!!!"

The humiliation I felt was just all too much.

I tried so hard! Why didn't he choose me? And Sara Hamilton of all people!!!! How could he have picked her and not me?? I even beat her in the race we had at training yesterday, so why didn't I make the team?

These thoughts raced wildly around and around in my head. I was so distraught, I couldn't lie still. Getting up off the bed, I began to pace around the room. This had meant everything to me but had been whipped away in the blink of an eye, when Mr. Thompson put up that list.

I couldn't bring myself to accept what had happened. It just wasn't fair!

A soft knocking on the door caught my attention and I heard my mother's voice. "Julia, are you ok?"

I didn't even know that she was home from work and wondered if she had heard me crying. But I did not feel at all like talking to her and announced through the closed door that I was fine.

The last thing I wanted was my mom telling me not to worry about it.

"Don't worry, Julia!" she would say. "You can try out again next year!"

As if that would make me feel any better!

I sat back down on my bed and stared into space. I felt miserable and just wanted to be left alone.

Then, as my vision came back into focus, I caught sight of the dream board on my wall. My first impulse was to rip it down and tear it to shreds.

It took almost superhuman strength to resist the urge to reach for it and do just that. I forced myself to take a deep breath. And then another and another. With my breathing finally at a steady rhythm, I began to feel calmer. It was then that I looked up at my dream board again.

My list of goals was staring down at me. The words I had carefully written and the scenes I had constantly visualized in my mind were all there.

"I am now on the school running team, competing in the regional event and I have won my race."

The decorated strip of paper where I had written that goal had been moved to the very center of the board and underneath it was the picture of me crossing in first place over the finish line.

I stared at the image and thought about the vision I had created many times already in my mind.

Then, almost like a light bulb glowing brightly in a darkened room, some familiar words flashed through my thoughts.

'The important thing is to never give up,'

I repeated those words in my head as I remembered where I had seen them written. It was in the book of dreams that I had read the previous year and the words had been repeated throughout in several places.

'Never give up!'

Sitting there, I considered that phrase. And then I was struck with another thought. I really had two choices.

The first choice was to focus on being miserable and dwell in self-pity. But where would that get me? Would it make me feel any better and would it change anything? I knew for certain, that you get what you focus on and if I continued dwelling on those negative thoughts, then I was doomed to misery.

Then I reflected on the alternative. I had worked so hard to achieve my goal. Was I really going to give up now? Hadn't I created several miracles already? Hadn't so many wonderful things happened to me since I had decided to be a more positive person? And wasn't the idea of a positive mindset much more rewarding than a negative one?

Suddenly I was struck with a fierce sense of determination. I desperately wanted to be on that team. I was going to make it happen and I didn't care what anyone said or thought. With that conviction in mind, I lay back on my bed and visualized the scene I was determined to create.

A short while later, I opened my bedroom door and went downstairs for dinner.

The surprise...

When I arrived at school the following morning, Millie, Blake, and Sara were nowhere to be seen. I guessed that they were still at their morning training session along with the others who had made the team. So I sat down at my desk and organized myself for our Math lesson.

Millie and Blake had both phoned me the night before, each of them saying how bad it was that I hadn't been chosen. I appreciated their support and was grateful that they cared enough to ring, but I didn't stay on the phone long and made excuses to end the calls fairly quickly. The truth was that I hadn't wanted to talk about not being selected. And I knew they'd think I was crazy if I told them what I was actually focusing on.

When I'd eventually confided all the details to my brother, Matt, as well as my goal to still be included in the tournament, he just looked at me in a weird way and shook his head. I knew he thought I was strange sometimes but I didn't care. After that, I decided to just keep my thoughts to myself.

The smirk on Sara's face as she entered the room that morning was directed towards me. Then she made a point of loudly sharing her news with our teacher.

"Miss Watson!" she had exclaimed. "Guess what! I made the running team! So I won't be at school on Friday because I'm competing in the regional tournament!"

It was incredible to watch…the manner in which she drew attention to herself as if she were the only one who mattered.

Millie, who had entered the room right behind her, quickly added, "Lots of us made the team, Sara. You weren't the only one!"

But this didn't bother Sara. She simply made her way to her desk at the back of the room and sat down with a proud grin.

I knew that she had every right to be proud though and I tried not to feel jealous. Then the friendly wave and warm smile that Blake gave me as he walked in the door was like an instant ray of sunshine and all my fears and concerns just seemed to melt away.

I reminded myself to feel thankful right then. I was so lucky to have Blake in my life as well as my best friend, Millie who had just sat down beside me. And with those thoughts in mind, I smiled gratefully and focused on the Math that Miss Watson had put on the board.

During our morning tea break, I caught sight of Mr. Thompson who nodded towards me in recognition. It appeared that he was heading in the direction of our group, and I assumed he needed to speak to Blake, Millie, and the others about the event that was scheduled for the coming Friday. However as he approached us, it was me he wanted to speak to.

"Julia," he said. "We've had a change of plan. Jodie Milford saw me this morning and apparently her grandmother is very ill, so her family is leaving tomorrow to spend time with her. They will probably be gone for several days and this means Jodie will not be here for the tournament."

I looked at him questioningly, trying to comprehend what he was saying to me.

"So now I'd like you to be our reserve runner. But I need you to realize that you'll only be going as a reserve, so you'll just be there as a back-up."

Instantly my hopes soared. "Oh my gosh, that's fine, Mr.

Thompson. I'm just happy to be going!" I could barely suppress my excitement and as he handed me the permission note, I simply stared at it in wonder. My goal was getting closer. I could feel it! And once again I pictured myself crossing first over the finish line.

Millie and Blake were overjoyed to hear that I would at least be able to attend the event with them but the look on Sara's face when I turned up for training the following morning showed that she obviously did not feel the same way.

Ignoring her, I joined the others on the track and focused on my goal as I ran.

"I've won the final race! I've won the final race! I've won the final race!"

I chanted the words in my head, over and over, all the while visualizing the image I wanted to create.

I knew that if Millie or Blake or any of the others knew what was going on in my mind, they would definitely think I had a mental problem. I chuckled with amusement at the thought of that and focused on my goal once more.

The tournament...

Finally, Friday arrived and we found ourselves at the tournament grounds. We were all in awe of the beautiful facilities that were available to us for the day. It was a professional track where serious athletes trained on a regular basis and it was suddenly clear to everyone that the competition was going to be strong.

I joined in with the others to do some warm-up exercises, thinking that I may as well be prepared. Sara's look of disdain had no effect on me and I could see that she was realizing this at last. I knew it was because she was not getting a reaction and would soon grow tired of trying.

Deep down, I was also aware that for some reason she felt an ongoing need to compete with me. Millie said it was because she was jealous, but I still couldn't understand why. Sara's parents gave her everything she ever asked for. She wore the nicest clothes of anyone in our grade. Everything she owned was expensive. She had a beautiful house and her family had heaps of money. And as well as that, she was really pretty. Of all people, I could not work out why she would be jealous of me!

But pushing those thoughts aside, I focused on what was important right then and tuned into what Mr. Thompson was saying. The boys' relay team event was scheduled first, followed by the boys' individual event. After that, the girls would compete.

As the boys headed over to the starting point to prepare for their race, we wished them luck and watched as they moved to their assigned spots around the track. Blake was the last runner because he was the fastest. Because Josh, the boys' sports captain, was the second-fastest runner in the team, he was the first to run. This was to help them get a good lead.

The instant the starting gun was fired, the crowd erupted. We joined in, cheering loudly as we watched the boys exchange the baton. Baton changes are tricky in a relay and everyone's biggest fear is that they might drop it and let the team down. But each of the boys' exchanges was perfect and we found ourselves jumping up and down in excitement as Blake grabbed hold of the baton and raced for the finish line.

"Go, Blake!!!! Go, Blake!!!! Go, Blake!!!!" We all chanted continuously and I could feel my stomach churn as he crept up behind the first place runner. They were almost neck and neck and the finish line was only about 75 feet away. Then all of a sudden, Blake had a burst of speed and like a bullet, he sped ahead to victory.

Squealing and screaming, we all went running over to him. It was one of the most exciting things I had ever witnessed and I was so happy to see him win.

The other boys raced over and started jumping on his back and hugging each other crazily. They were completely overcome with the thrill of winning, especially after all their hard work, but it had certainly been worth it. We stood back cheering them once more as they headed to the judges' tent to claim their medals.

The next races were run by older age groups so we joined the boys under the shelter where we'd stored all our gear then admired the medals and ribbons they'd been presented with. We only hoped that the girls' team could do as well as the boys had.

Before too long, the boys were called for the individual races and were organized into heats. Blake and Josh had to run in the same race which meant they'd be competing against each other. But with a friendly rivalry, they wished each other luck and lined up to run.

It was awesome to see that both of them had made the finals and it was an incredible effort for two of our boys to get that far. It was even more amazing though, to see Blake come in second in the final event and that was when I got the chance to hug him proudly. I was thrilled that he had done so well and was also extremely grateful that I'd been given the opportunity to be there to watch.

Before long, it was time for the girls' relay and I walked over to the sideline with the boys so we could cheer them on. At the last minute, however, Mr. Thompson swapped their order, but we really weren't sure why.

He had decided to place Millie in the first runner position and Sara in the last. And we watched anxiously as the gun was fired and the runners all took off. Millie had an incredible start and our team was in the lead. Jumping up and down excitedly, we cheered on as we watched the smooth baton changes where the girls grabbed hold of the metal tube and ran like the wind. It seemed that Amy's timing was really fast as she gained distance on the runner behind her. Then with the speed of lightning, she raced towards Sara, who was ready for her turn to run.

Reaching out to grasp the baton, Sara started running, the way we had practiced so many times at training. We could see her focusing on taking a firm hold of the shiny metal but just as her hands wrapped around it, she seemed to stumble. Looking on in horror, we watched as the baton fell to the ground.

"Nooooo!!!" we screamed in disbelief, knowing that dropping the baton meant instant disqualification. And as Sara bent down to pick it up, the other teams raced past her.

Hobbling over to our tent, she collapsed into a chair red-faced with shame.

"I twisted my ankle!" she declared furiously as we all approached her.

"It's not my fault, the stupid track is uneven. It's dangerous! Surely they could make sure the track is safe before letting us run here!"

"Never mind, Sara," Amy responded quietly. She was obviously very disappointed but resisted the temptation to blame Sara for the loss.

It was clear that they would have been sure winners if Sara had not dropped that baton. They had practiced the exchanges so many times, there really was no excuse. But what point was there in freaking out at her. It wouldn't achieve anything now.

It was then that Millie stated the obvious. "If you've hurt your ankle then you're not going to be able to run in the individual races!"

The realization of that statement abruptly dawned on Sara's face.

"Oh, I'll be fine," she quickly replied. "It actually feels ok now, it barely hurts at all."

"No, Sara," interrupted Mr. Thompson who had just joined us and overheard Sara's comments.

"I don't want you to risk doing more damage to your ankle. We'll get it checked by the first aid officer just to be sure, but you won't be running again today."

Looking towards me he then said, "Julia, you'd better get warmed up, because you'll be running in the individual race. And the heats are due to start in about fifteen minutes."

With that, he took off to find a medical officer to look at Sara's foot. And, standing riveted to the spot in shock, I gradually comprehended the scene around me.

Shaking me into awareness, Millie grabbed my arm and said, "Come on, Julia! Let's get you warmed up. You've got a race to run!"

Trying to process what had actually happened right then, I spotted the look of envy and disgust from Sara, who sat there shaking her head in disbelief.

But Millie dragged me away so quickly that Sara's evil stare was whisked into oblivion and I had no time to think about it further.

Still in shock at the unexpected turn of events, I lined up alongside several other girls for the heats and with my heart racing a million miles per minute, I suddenly found myself taking off at the sound of the gun. Keeping stride with the girl next to me all the way around the track, I noticed her picking up speed and she then raced ahead, making it to the finish line in first place. Panting, I managed to come in a very close second and after pausing for breath, we made our way to the judges' tent.

But we had an agonizing wait for all the other heats to be over before we could find out which girls had made the finals.

Sitting alongside Blake and the others, we waited impatiently for the names to be called and when they announced Amy Mitchell and Julia Jones amongst several other names, I sat there in shock. Although over the moon to be in the final, the way I had dreamed, I felt bad for Millie and looked at her almost guiltily.

"Oh, my gosh! You are in the finals, Julia. This is insane!!!" Millie was beside herself with genuine admiration and I looked at her gratefully. She was the best friend anyone could wish for and right then, she meant more to me than ever!

"Girls, this is an incredible effort! I'm extremely proud of all of you. Now, Amy and Julia just go and do your best!" Mr. Thompson was beaming at us and I was overjoyed to be given the chance to run again.

A short while later, Amy and I lined up and waited for the signal to move towards the starting line, from where I could see Blake and the others standing expectantly at the finish.

"Good luck, Julia!" he had said earlier. "You'll kill it!" And he'd given me a quick hug of encouragement before going to join the others. Then I had taken my place in the line.

In those few moments before the gun went off, the scene around me felt surreal. I had pictured it so many times in my mind, but I found it difficult to believe that it was actually happening.

Looking around in wonder, I wanted to pinch myself to make sure I was in fact actually standing at the start of the final race. But the loud blast from the gun ensured me that it was definitely real and then, almost as if I had no control whatsoever, my legs began to move.

Racing along the track, side by side with the other runners, I could feel the blood pumping through my veins while my shoes pounded the ground beneath me. Thump! Thump! Thump!

The wind whipped my hair back and my legs ran on and on. With every step, I could feel the hammering of my heart and it became more intense with every stride.

The screaming from the crowd was deafening, but I blocked everything from my senses. Everything except the pound of my legs and arms and the feel of the track under my feet, as I pushed myself forwards. Nothing existed except that moment, and rounding the last bend, I saw the finish line come clearly into view.

There were two competitors slightly ahead of me, their pace steady and fast. With the finish line dead ahead, within my sights and within reach, it was my last chance. If only I could just push a little harder.

On and on I ran, with my lungs about to burst. Then, with a millisecond to spare, I grasped desperately to my last reserve of energy. Striding forward with a rush of speed, it was as though my legs had wings. And as I raised my arms in triumph, I sped across the finish line in first place.

On impulse, I glanced to my right and there looking directly at me, was the most beautiful smile in the whole universe. It was the proudest moment of my life and the best part was that I had him to share it with at the end. More grateful than ever, I ran towards him, my heart bursting with pride and joy.

"Julia! Julia! You did it!!!" And as I watched him speak those words and open his arms wide in a huge embrace, I realized it was his smile that was the best part of all.

Find out what lies ahead for Julia and all her friends in

Book 5

My Life is Great!

***

Thank you so much for reading my book.

If you liked it and have time to leave a review, that would be awesome!

Thank you!

Katrina x

Follow Julia Jones on Instagram @juliajonesdiary

And please LIKE Julia Jones' Diary Facebook page to be kept up to date with all our latest books...

https://www.facebook.com/JuliaJonesDiary

Introducing a brand new series…

Mind Reader – Book 1:
My New Life

OUT NOW!!

This book introduces Emmie, a girl who unexpectedly arrives in Carindale and meets Millie. But Emmie has a secret, a secret that must remain hidden at all costs.

What happens to Julia, Blake, Sara and all the others and how does Emmie's sudden appearance affect Julia and her friends?

This fabulous new series continues the story of Julia Jones but has a whole new twist, one that all Julia Jones' Diary fans are sure to enjoy.

If you like reading about kids with special powers, I'm sure you'll also love to read

THE SECRET

The story of a boy with a completely different type of power. And when a very pretty girl moves in next door, his life starts to get REALLY complicated!

Available Now!

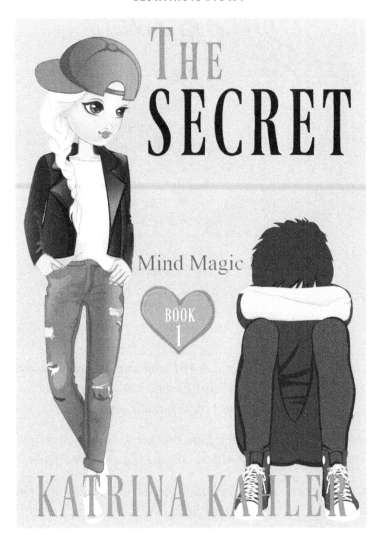

Announcing ANOTHER New Series!

Exciting News! Katrina Kahler has continued to tell the story of Julia Jones - 3 years on - yes, the Teenage Years. Julia is older, but is she wiser? Whatever happened to Blake and Sara?

Grab the first new book in the series now! You'll love it!

Julia Jones – The Teenage Years

Book 1: Falling Apart

Out NOW!

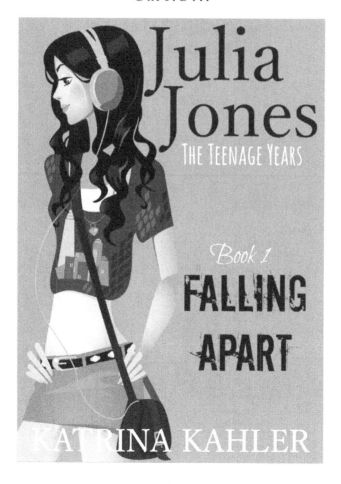

Here are some other books that I'm sure you will enjoy reading...

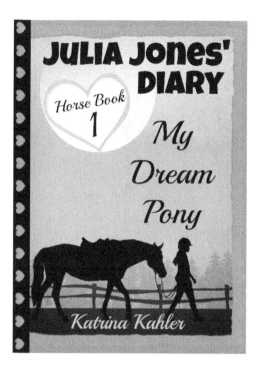

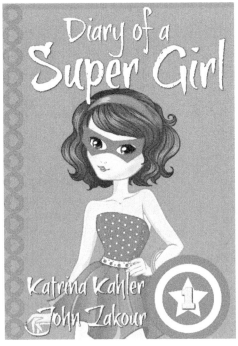

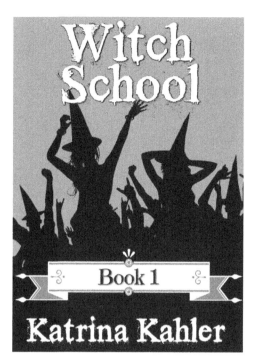

Made in the USA
Columbia, SC
25 November 2020

25426521R20065